For Johnny and Chloe

little bee books

An imprint of Bonnier Publishing Group
853 Broadway, New York, New York 10003
Text and illustration copyright © 2015 by Sally Garland.
First published in the United Kingdom by Top That Publishing Ltd.
This little bee books edition, 2015.
All rights reserved, including the right of reproduction in whole
or in part in any form. LITTLE BEE BOOKS is a trademark of
Bonnier Publishing Group.
Manufactured in Guangdong, China 1014 HH
First Edition 2 4 6 8 10 9 7 5 3 1
Library of Congress Control Number: 2015934161
ISBN 978-1-4998-0155-2

www.littlebeebooks.com
www.bonnierpublishing.com

Tig & Tog's Dinosaur Discovery

by Sally Garland

little bee books

Tig and Tog are best friends.
But sometimes, even best friends
have trouble sharing.

Tig didn't want Tog to play with the
stick they found.

It was her stick.

So she stomped away and sat alone, drawing in the snow with it.

Then Tig noticed something strange
sticking out of the ground.

She used her stick to scrape
and scratch the dirt.

But the stick wasn't enough!

She needed something else to dig it out of the ground.

"Maybe this will help?"
said Tog.

Tog took a spoon out of his pocket, and he sat down to dig. Tig was glad to have her friend's help.

With the spoon, they scooped
the dirt. But it was no good.

The spoon wasn't enough!

They still needed something
else to dig the thing out
of the ground.

In the sandbox, Tig and Tog
found a little plastic shovel.

With the little shovel they dug and dug.

But even the shovel wasn't enough!

They still needed something else
to dig the thing out of the ground.

Tig and Tog looked for
something else to help
them dig.

Looking around,
they saw a bucket
in a muddy puddle.

Tog pulled it out using the stick.

Tig and Tog took turns filling the bucket with dirt and tipping it out.

But even the bucket wasn't enough!

They still needed something else to dig the thing out of the ground.

"Can you see
what it is yet?"

asked Tig.

'It's so strange
and big! What
do you think
it is?"

"It looks like white stones, but it's too long to be stones!"

said Tog.

"Let's keep digging and find out,"

said Tig and Tog together.

After a lot of searching,
Tig and Tog found a
wheelbarrow . . .

. . . and a BIG shovel.

With the big shovel, Tig and Tog were able to dig deeper, and they could move more dirt with the wheelbarrow.

But even the wheelbarrow and shovel weren't enough!

They *still* needed something else to dig the thing out of the ground.

All day long Tig and Tog
worked together, using
the tools they had found.

They scratched, scooped, dug, tipped,
and shoveled the dirt.

But even with all these tools and all their hard work, they still needed something else to dig the thing out of the ground!

Suddenly, Tog had an excellent idea!
Leaving Tig scratching her head,
Tog soon returned with a big yellow digger!

With three mighty shovels,
the digger cleared the dirt!

Tig and Tog both looked
in amazement at what they
had found . . .

It was the most ENORMOUS
dinosaur skeleton!

And the stick?

Tig decided to share it with Tog.
After all, she couldn't have made
the discovery without him.

From that day on, the two friends
always shared everything.